On Poppy's Beach

WRITTEN BY
Susan Pynn Taylor

ILLUSTRATED BY
David Sturge

We gratefully acknowledge the financial support of the Canada Council for the Arts, the Government of Canada through the Canada Book Fund (CBF), and the Government of Newfoundland and Labrador through the Department of Tourism, Culture and Recreation for our publishing program.

Illustrations and book design by David Sturge
Printed on acid-free paper

Published by
TUCKAMORE BOOKS
an imprint of CREATIVE BOOK PUBLISHING
a Transcontinental Inc. associated company
P.O. Box 8660, Stn. A
St. John's, Newfoundland and Labrador A1B 3T7

Printed in Canada

2nd Printing, 2015
3rd Printing, 2016

Library and Archives Canada Cataloguing in Publication

Taylor, Susan, 1960-, author
    On Poppy's beach / Susan Taylor & David Sturge.

ISBN 978-1-77103-015-1 (pbk.)

I. Sturge, David, 1961-, illustrator II. Title.

PS8639.A964O5 2013   jC813'.6   C2013-905568-1

On Poppy's Beach

For my two beautiful sons, Jacob and Stephen - in joyful memory of childhood days
featuring beach rocks, sand, sea, and sometimes, jellyfish. With a gentle reminder that
no matter how old you get, I love you both forever - and with all my heart. Mom.

David would like to dedicate this book to his friends and family for their support
and most of all to his great-nephew, Grady Monahan Saunders
for being his inspiration.

On Poppy's beach

the seagulls call.

A few more lazy

raindrops fall.

The tide runs low,

the sun climbs high,

as fog slips from

the harbour sky.

On Poppy's beach
I sniff the air
as breezes softly
tease my hair.
It smells so fresh
and salty too,
all tangled with
the morning dew.

On Poppy's beach
the brown sand warms.
A cotton-candy
rainbow forms.
The ocean sparkles
diamond bright
below the fluff-puff
clouds of white.

On Poppy's beach
a boat I see.
The fishermen
wave back at me.
They're checking all
their lobster traps,
and bringing in
the morning catch.

On Poppy's beach

a small crab peeks.

I pop some seaweed

and it squeaks.

While silent in

the cool, blue sea,

a jellyfish

looks up at me.

On Poppy's beach

a wave rolls in

and wets my toes,

but I just grin.

I stoop to greet

a pink starfish

and close my eyes

to make a wish.

On Poppy's beach
I watch the spray
of humpbacks breeching
in the bay,
a school of dolphins
laughing too,
while playing games
of peek-a-boo.

On Poppy's beach
seashells I find.
My bucket's filled
with every kind.
I keep the ones
I like the best,
to hide home in
my treasure chest.

On Poppy's beach
he mends his nets
and just before
the gold sun sets,
I build a castle
with a moat,
as Poppy warms me
with his coat.

On Poppy's beach
the tide gets higher
as friends start up
a driftwood fire.
While Poppy fiddles,
I play spoons
to I'se the B'y
and other tunes.

On Poppy's beach

our neighbours' lips

tell tales of mermaids,

pirate ships...

I've seen them

only in a book,

but, just in case,

I sneak a look.

On Poppy's beach
stars peep and glow.
My eyes are closing,
far below.
The moonrise lights
us all about
but I don't want
to leave - I pout.

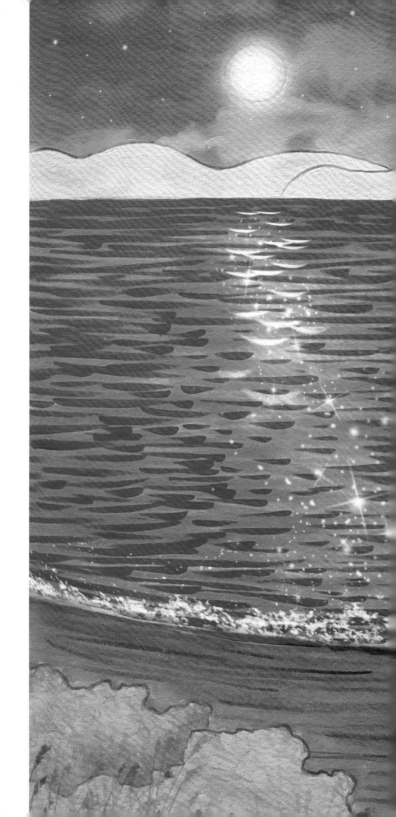

On Poppy's beach
it's getting colder...
rest my head
on momma's shoulder.
Hugs for Poppy
and for Nan.
I say, "I'll come back
when I can."

I wave goodnight
and though I'm small,

such happy times
I will recall

and cherish still

when out of reach -

these childhood days

on Poppy's beach.

A native Newfoundlander, Susan Pynn Taylor is a professional writer with a background in marketing and communications. She has traveled all over North America, but always finds her way back to her island home. A devoted wife and mother, Susan has a love for children, literature, and nature. On Poppy's Beach is her fourth book for young readers.

David Sturge is a graphic designer and illustrator who was born and raised in St. John's, Newfoundland where he currently resides. He studied commercial art and graphic design at The College of The North Atlantic and is currently working as a designer in the advertising and marketing industry. David is very excited to work on this, his first illustration project for Tuckamore Books.